JUN   2017

Grandma D's Bubbles

A Lesson in Life and Loss

Debra Joy Hart

AuthorHouse™
1663 Liberty Drive
Bloomington, IN 47403
www.authorhouse.com
Phone: 1-800-839-8640

Published by AuthorHouse: 01/08/2015

ISBN: 978-1-4969-6195-2 (sc)
ISBN: 978-1-4969-6196-9 (e)

Library of Congress Control Number: 2014922959

This book is printed on acid-free paper.

Because of the dynamic nature of the Internet, any web addresses or links contained in this book may have changed since publication and may no longer be valid. The views expressed in this work are solely those of the author and do not necessarily reflect the views of the publisher, and the publisher hereby disclaims any responsibility for them.

authorHOUSE®

With Gratitude and Love,
Husband Unit: Darrell Hart
Illustrator and Red Ribbon Trails
(FCAN) camp buddy: Caitlin Yates
Editors and friends:
Judy Hoffman, Kate Grueneberg, Joel Schwartz,
Cheryl Brown, Steve Wilson, Catherine Novak
Grandchildren extraordinaire:
Sophia, Josiah, Claire, Judah, Austin and Evy
And Dawn Williams
(Harold, Jeannie and Kara).
Her death inspired this story.

Grandma D was sitting outside on her steps with a new package of bubbles.

Some people thought Grandma D was too old and too silly to play with bubbles.

But she didn't care. She liked them…
in fact she LOVED playing with bubbles.

Sophia loved that Grandma D liked to be silly. Sophia liked to be silly too. Sometimes being silly made Sophia feel better. Like the time when her goldfish died. That day, Sophia went over to Grandma D's house. Sophia said to Grandma D in a sad voice, "My fishy died."

Grandma D gave her a hug. Sophia said, "Mommy and I said goodbye to my fishy, wrapped him in paper towel and put him in a box. Then we put him in the garbage can." Grandma D said, "Now Fishy gets to ride on a garbage truck…which would be fun."

Grandma D and Sophia laughed. Laughing made Sophia feel better about the loss of her fishy.

One day, Sophia and her Mommy came over and Grandma D had just opened up a new package of bubbles.

Sophia was really quiet. She looked sad and not her usual silly, happy self.

Sophia's Mommy said to Grandma D, "Sophia's Auntie died." Grandma D just nodded.

Grandma D remembered when her own Auntie died and how sad she had felt. No one had known what to say to Grandma D to make her feel better. Grandma D wondered if Sophia felt that way too.

Grandma D asked Sophia to come outside, and sit on the steps.

Grandma D started blowing bubbles and talking. Sophia sat quietly next to Grandma D.

"The first part about making bubbles is everyone needs a magic bubble wand." Grandma D showed the wand to Sophia. "The next part is bubble juice. The bubble juice is just like life. Sometimes it drips. Sometimes it makes a mess. And, everyone needs bubble juice to make bubbles." Sophia watched the bubble juice drip.

"Another important part of making bubbles is breath. A breath blows the bubbles. I take a breath in, blow out through the wand, and watch the bubbles float by.

Sometimes the bubbles don't work and I get to try again."

"When I try to catch a bubble,
some are out of reach.
Sometimes the bubbles pop."

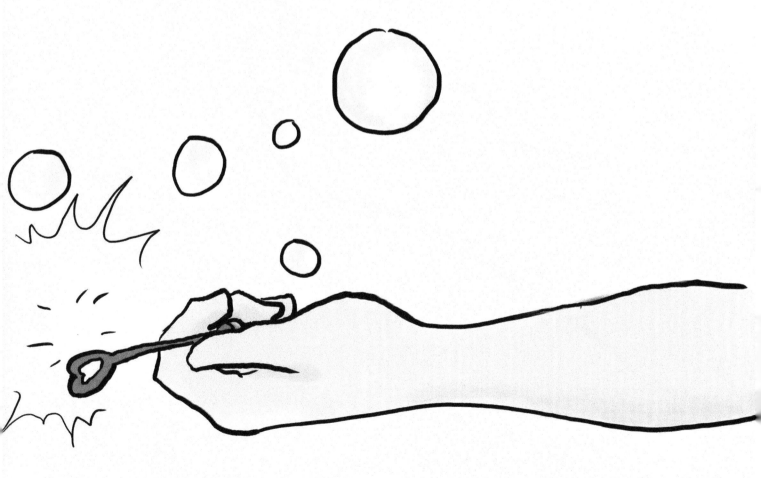

"I take another breath in, and then I blow again to make more bubbles."

"I catch a bubble and look at all the pretty, swirling colors. I like when the colors move and change."

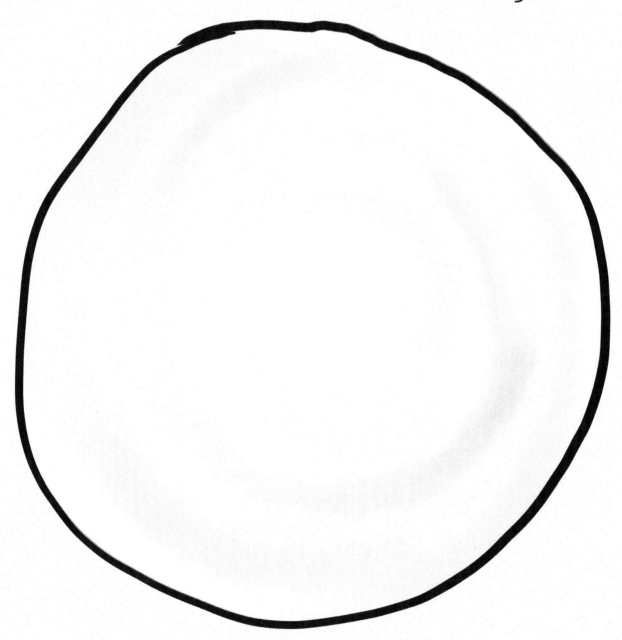

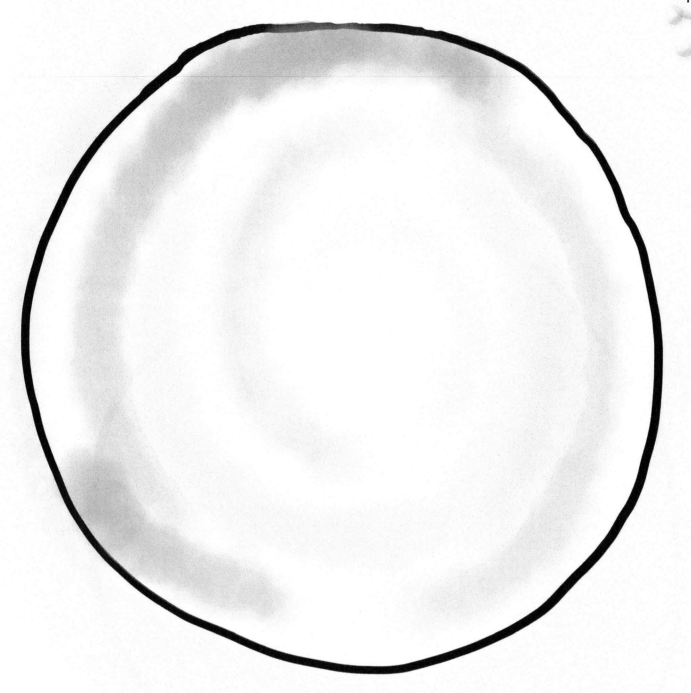

"There is pink and blue and green and yellow… like a round bubble rainbow."

"Then the colors fade."

"The bubble looks grey."

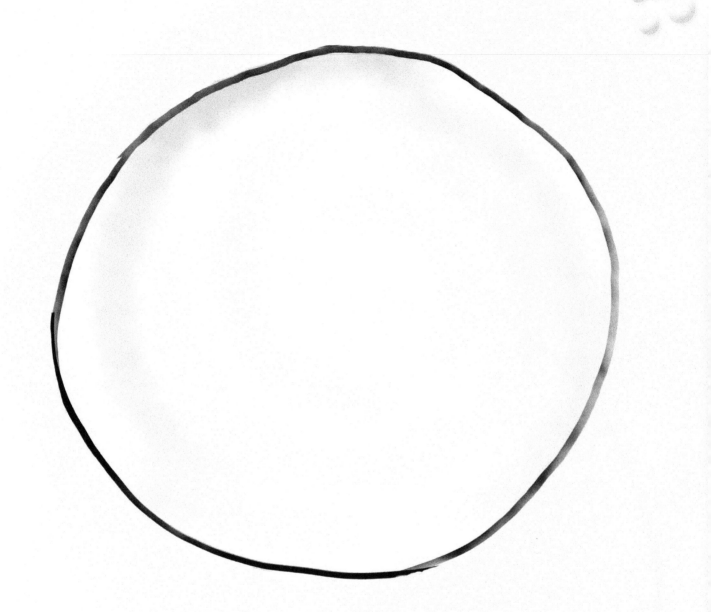

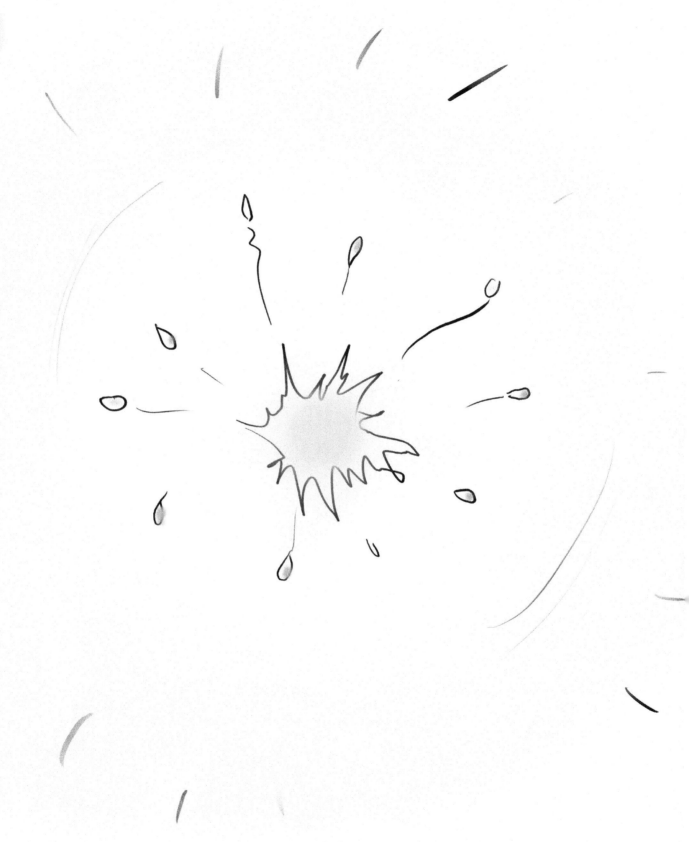

"Then the bubble pops."

Grandma D stopped talking and began blowing a lot of bubbles as fast as she could.

It looked like Grandma D was filling the sky with bubbles. The bubbles started to land on Grandma D and Sophia. Some bubbles popped, and others floated away until they could no longer see them.

Grandma D said to Sophia, "Bubbles are like the people and animals we love. Some are big and some are little. Some bubbles last longer than others and I love them all. When the bubble pops a little bubble juice gets on me. I call that a bubble kiss!"

Sophia smiled.

"Just like people and dogs and cats and even goldfish," said Grandma D. "All bubbles are beautiful and precious. They are made up of many colors and are perfect in their own way. All have air and love around them. All have air and love within them."

"When a bubble pops, or a person or dog or cat or even a goldfish dies, their air and love remain. Their air and love will help us blow new bubbles, see new colors and watch new bubbles pop. That means more bubble kisses!"

Grandma D looked and Sophia was smiling.

"I don't feel sad anymore," said Sophia. "Can I blow some bubbles?"

Grandma D said," Will you give me bubble kisses?"

Sophia laughed." Grandma D you are so silly."

And Grandma D laughed too.

CPSIA information can be obtained
at www.ICGtesting.com
Printed in the USA
LVOW06s1658090517

533890LV00020B/375/P